The Eight Nights of Chanukah

BY *Lesléa Newman* ILLUSTRATED BY *Elivia Savadier*

Harry N. Abrams, Inc., Publishers

On the first night of Chanukah
I clap my hands to see . . .

A present waiting for me.

On the second night of Chanukah
I clap my hands to see
Two Maccabees
And a present waiting for me.

On the third night of Chanukah
I clap my hands to see
Three challahs
Two Maccabees
And a present waiting for me.

On the fourth night of Chanukah
I clap my hands to see
Four matzo balls
Three challahs
Two Maccabees
And a present waiting for me.

On the fifth night of Chanukah
I clap my hands to see
Five bags of gelt
Four matzo balls
Three challahs
Two Maccabees
And a present waiting for me.

On the sixth night of Chanukah
I clap my hands to see
Six dreidels spinning
Five bags of gelt
Four matzo balls
Three challahs
Two Maccabees
And a present waiting for me.

On the seventh night of Chanukah
I clap my hands to see
Seven latkes frying
Six dreidels spinning
Five bags of gelt
Four matzo balls
Three challahs
Two Maccabees
And a present waiting for me.

On the eighth night of Chanukah
I clap my hands to see
Eight maidels dancing
Seven latkes frying
Six dreidels spinninng
Five bags of gelt
Four matzo balls
Three challahs
Two Maccabees

And a present waiting for me.

Note

Chanukah (sometimes spelled Hanukkah, Hannukah or Hanukah) is the eight-day Jewish holiday that celebrates the rededication of the Temple of Jerusalem by the Maccabees. In 175 BCE, King Antiochus IV of Syria ruled over Judea and the Jewish people. Among his many decrees, the king insisted that the Jews worship the Greek gods. This made the Jewish people very angry. A man named Mattathias and his five sons formed a group whom today we call the Maccabees. They were a small but determined group that fought King Antiochus and his army for several years. Eventually the Maccabees regained Jerusalem and drove the Syrians from the land!

When the Maccabees reached the great temple in Jerusalem, they discovered it had been nearly destroyed by the Syrians. The great seven-branched menorah, meant to burn day and night, stood dark and neglected. The Maccabees cleaned the temple and built a new altar. They discovered there was very little holy oil—not enough to keep the menorah burning until more could be found. Yet when they lit the menorah, a miracle occurred: the oil which should have been gone before the day was out burned bright for eight days, until more holy oil arrived.

In Hebrew, Chanukah means "rededication." It is a holiday of light, feasting, fun—and gifts!

Glossary

 **Challah**: braided egg bread eaten on the Jewish Sabbath and Festival Days.

 Dreidel: a square-sided spinning top traditionally played with during Chanukah, decorated with the Hebrew letters "nun," "gimel," "hey," and "shin," which stand for "A Great Miracle Happened There."

Gelt: money; also commonly refers to the thin chocolate coins wrapped in gold foil traditionally given to children on Chanukah.

 **Latke**: a potato pancake, traditionally eaten on Chanukah.

 **Maccabees**: a group of Jewish fighters led by Judah Maccabee, who recaptured the Temple of Jerusalem from King Antiochus in the year 164 BCE.

 Maidel: a girl.

Matzo Ball: a dumpling made of matzo meal, tradionally served in chicken soup.

   **Menorah**: a candle holder with places for seven, eight, or nine candles. A Chanukah menorah (also called a Chanukiah) holds nine candles, one for each of the eight nights of Chanukah and one for the shamash, or "helper candle," which is used to light all the others. In ancient times, menorahs were oil lamps. Today, most menorahs use candles.

For Tzivia, Chris, and Miranda
—L.N.

For Jenny and Jasper because of the hat, and Isabel for your love of life!
—E.S.

Medium: Ink pen line with watercolor washes

Designed by Edward Miller
Production Manager: Jonathan Lopes

Library of Congress Cataloging-in-Publication Data has been applied for.
ISBN 0-8109-5785-X
Text copyright © 2005 Lesléa Newman
Illustrations copyright © 2005 Elivia Savadier

Printed and bound in U.S.A.
10 9 8 7 6 5 4 3 2

Harry N. Abrams, Inc.
100 Fifth Avenue
New York, NY 10011
www.abramsbooks.com

Abrams is a subsidiary of

LA MARTINIÈRE
GROUPE